The Future is Brief

The Future is Brief

Jean-Paul L. Garnier

ISBN 979-8-9896308-4-4
First Edition | 2024
Cover art - The Grotto by Randy Polumbo

Space Cowboy Books
61871 29 Palms Hwy.
Joshua Tree, CA 92252
www.spacecowboybooks.com

Introduction

The Shadows May Lengthen in Carcosa, but the Future is Brief

By Denise Dumars

What is scifaiku? Let me start my introduction to Jean-Paul Garnier's selection of scifaiku in *The Future is Brief* with words from someone we both knew who is better at defining scifaiku than I am:

"I find that the speculative haiku which work best are those where the speculative image juxtaposes with my everyday life or recounts something that actually happened to me in a speculative way.

the tug
of a black hole
this isolation
#FemkuMag, April 2020

"The tug of a black hole" is a speculative image, but "this isolation" — written in the time of the pandemic and stay-at-home orders — means that while this poem is a "speculative haiku" about a black hole, it also can be read as a pandemic haiku."—Deborah P. Kolodji, "New to Haiku—Advice for Beginners," The Haiku Foundation, 9 Jan. 2022, https://thehaikufoundation.org/new-to-haiku-advice-for-beginners-deborah-p-kolodji/

The fascinating thing to me is that a scifaiku like the one above falls strictly within the classic definition of haiku in that it has its inspiration in nature: nature encompassing all creation, and all destruction as well. But haiku that deals mostly with human activity, especially that which is wryly funny or dark or sometimes both, is categorized as senryu. I'll leave it to the reader as to whether Garnier's poems are mostly scifaiku or SFnal senryu; the definition, of course, is not as important as the poems themselves and what they say and mean. And no, haiku does not have to always be three lines of 5/7/5 syllables; that's just silly.

Garnier has divided the scifaiku into thematic sections: First, *Time*, probably the best scientifically slippery topic and also most traditional for this type of poem; this is followed by *Transhumanism*, the most hands-on of these scientific concepts; *Space*, our classic topic in Science Fiction; *Aliens and Robots*, our classic tropes within this topic; and finally *Science*, which is, after all, the "Sci" is Scifaiku.

But sometimes these poems do more than embody a snapshot, as does the traditional haiku. There is, for one thing, allusion and explication in some of the poems, which may or may not be considered traditional. When is a haiku more than a haiku? When it is more than a haiku, does the haiku that it is cease to exist? I'll leave that for the reader, for as with all poetry, haiku is a collaboration between the writer and the reader.

The examples that mean the most to me are those that do what Kolodji does in her example. From the first section, this one:

a plastic plant
symbol of human hubris as
the last tree dies

I can say so much about this small poem, and also show how it demonstrates another aspect of most haiku, whether SFnal or not: the turn, or the place in which the poem utilizes a *kireji,* a word that indicated the juxtaposition of two different ideas or images. In this case, the poem pivots on the word "as." "A plastic plant/symbol of human hubris" is one statement;

"as/the last tree dies" is another, but the first hinges upon the second to make the point of the poem. So for me, this poem typifies not only Kolodji's point, but also the point that writers of haiku including scifaiku (and horrorku) want to make.

A seasonal reference is generally what we look for in haiku; does scifaiku need to demonstrate that as well? Maybe, maybe not. As in much mainstream haiku, a reference to nature often seems to suffice, and, speaking of which, do we always have to be so serious? Remember, even Basho had a poem about horse pee, so perhaps not! I laughed out loud at the following haiku from the *Transhumanism* section:

> I grafted myself to the
> branches of a tree
> was always a fruit

This bit of silliness got me to thinking about actual grafting and the way that, long before we had fancy things like genetic engineering, our ancestors were creating new hybrids. And then the double meaning of "fruit" which of course is what makes the poem funny. Does the poem also have a seasonal reference? You tell me.

From *Time* and *Transhumanism* we go to *Space*. Are there seasons in space? Uh, I guess it depends. But the glory of nature is definitely there, as with more earthly haiku:

> beautiful sunsets
> in tertiary systems
> three for every night

A new non-problem for the three-body problem, perhaps. But humanity has always been fascinated and thrilled by the beauty of the cosmos, and only recently have we been able to see beyond our unaided senses. Science fiction is often about the awe a person would feel in encountering the marvelous in space, and "beautiful sunsets" is simply a tiny part of it, that haiku snapshot.

One of science fiction's greatest themes is imagining how aliens may differ from earth species. Under *Aliens and Robots*, we see several scifaiku examples, such as this one:

> music for the eyes a
> foreign race with no ears
> hears architecture

And how would an alien's senses differ from our own? I love this haiku not so much for its haikuness, if that's a word, but for its jumbling of the senses, trying to make sense of the senses that an alien race might demonstrate. So much here to discuss, and all in a tiny little poem.

As is common for contemporary science fiction, the science in "Science" tends toward the dystopian. That in itself is a kind of real-life *kireji*; science fiction was once intended to express wonder and amazement just as advancing science evoked the same emotions. Where did it all go wrong? You won't find much in the way of hopepunk in the scifaiku in this section of his book, but you will find beauty, and a reference to another Japanese art form:

> warp drive folds spacetime
> origami universe
> unseen from outside

Like science fiction in general, this scifaiku asks us to consider a scientific idea. How do we see the unseen? What would warp drive look like? The word "origami" itself gives the reader something to hold onto from the real world while the poem itself asks us to imagine something that, so far at least, does not exist.

I think you will enjoy these poems. They present so much to think about, which sort of puts the lie to the idea of haiku as a "snapshot." After all, even in an old Polaroid picture you can see something different, something more, every time you look at it. I think you'll have the same kind of experience with the poetry in *The Future is Brief*. Tiny snapshots, like the impossibly dense and impossibly small black holes. So much in so little!

Let's just hope the real future is not brief, at all. Garnier's work is for the ages.

TIME

vacuum energy
particles traverse all time
directions fluid

∞

revived dinosaur
Lazarus of a past age
finds meat but no mate

younger and older
selves meet up for the first time
and cannot relate

∞

granddad paradox
my twin and I plan murder
family tree mess

exhale Shiva's breath
cosmological timeframe
expansion speeds up

∞

geologic time
meet me for lunch when mountains
crumble and join seas

a plastic plant
symbol of human hubris
as the last tree dies

∞

beneath the glacier
the iceman begins to thaw
awakes in terror

the future police
arrest before crimes happen
temporal fascists

∞

seething virtual
particles travel in time
something for nothing

books are time machines
a form of telepathy
and magic made real

∞

anti-universe
contemporaneously
simultaneous

crumbling mountains
slow geological time
no human witness

∞

falling through the void
no reference point in sight
time irrelevant

last day of the Earth
isn't there anything else
on Television

∞

burning books for heat
hell came first, before the freeze
forget and stay warm

time freezes in light
waiting becomes redundant
all moments present

∞

event horizon
time forever at a standstill
halts the Universe

memories gather
time equals dark energy
cumulative space

∞

only time will tell
if the flow is linear
forward or backward

next time, if you please
wall me up on the side with
all that lovely wine

∞

younger twin returns
sibling aged and alone
lonely space proven

reality froze
severe glitch in the system
no reset button

∞

frozen, time stands still
it's gonna be a long wait
while we circulate

instantaneous
weight loss, on smaller planets
all the fashion rage

Ω

enter the hive mind
you will never be alone
now that you are us

new eyes that can see
entire EM spectrum
blinded by brightness

Ω

cybernetic code
tampering with evidence
biological

taste for the future
with resentment for the past
balances present

∞

the chronometer
tells the truth relatively
can it be trusted?

teleportation
always arriving early
unfashionable

∞

frogs busy boiling
come on in the water's nice
enjoy as Rome falls

revived ancient thing
displeased with oxygen
tries to roar but can't

∞

a hole opened up
revealing the hollow Earth's
monsters of the past

time machine broken
electronics era
predates industrial

∞

past self
passes by
young forever

TRANSHUMANISM

universe heat death
hadn't really thought through my
immortality

Ω

transhumanism
the machine and I become
much more than we were

our telepaphone
never a busy signal
free long distance too

Ω

I grafted myself
to the branches of a tree
was always a fruit

telepaths clouded
mind ever full of clatter
craves isolation

Ω

rewire the body
to go into outer space
need alterations

new eyes that can see
entire EM spectrum
blinded by brightness

Ω

cybernetic code
tampering with evidence
biological

instantaneous
weight loss, on smaller planets
all the fashion rage

Ω

enter the hive mind
you will never be alone
now that you are us

memory implant
and now the trauma does not
ever fade with time

Ω

the fountain of youth
take just one sip and you are
naïve forever

reading minds like books
Sturgeon's Law, much more schlock
than one could ever want

Ω

immortality
vanity's main desire
goes on for too long

SPACE

now invisible
feeling awkward and naked
the formula works

Ω

jaded with access
the computer mind bored
by information

the mind uploaded
unencumbered by the flesh
immortality

Ω

metamorphosis
shedding my skin, my own flesh
must also change mind

our minds unified
seek solitude once again
at peace without words

now invisible
feeling awkward and naked
the formula works

Ω

jaded with access
the computer mind bored
by information

the mind uploaded
unencumbered by the flesh
immortality

Ω

metamorphosis
shedding my skin, my own flesh
must also change mind

our minds unified
seek solitude once again
at peace without words

SPACE

a meteor trail
colors show composition
ancient stardust falls

☼

tidally locked
the poor all live in the dark side
cold permanent night

in need of shore leave
cramped traveling starship
no waters, no shore

☼

asteroid enroute
miners working double time
mass equals mass death

candle burns both ends
fire in zero gravity
burning up and down

☼

raining meteors
a global mass-extinction
clears way for new life

eruptions on Mars
vulcanism not active
nuclear warfare

☼

lame phallic symbols
machine size won't change manhood
rocket going limp

supernova death
we should have seen it coming
as the star bloated

☼

meteorite strike
through the skull into the brain
thinking about space

tidally locked
those of us in poverty
never see twilight

☼

reluctant spacemen
leaving Earth against their will
off to space prison

burnup reentry
atmospheric conditions
thick and harsh return

☼

artificial moons
imprison us on the Earth
a cage of space junk

dead on the launchpad
the dream meets impotent death
before leaving Earth

☼

hexagonal storms
geometry of the eye
metallic rains come

in dark moon craters
frozen waters could revive
spacemen water bears

☼

radiation bath
ice skating on Europa
worth a shorter life

bombardment era
churning stone into landscape
emulate with bombs

☼

a small mote of dust
ever falling through grand space
the Earth so lonely

the ice cracks slowly
surface virgin, delicate
not for mankind's boot

☼

a sphere of water
floating majestic, serene
electronics fry

final earth sunrise
supernova imminent
the last of our days

☼

alien microbe
a cellular division
pestilence unleashed

danger, bingo fuel
alone in the black ocean
forever floating

☼

with the inflation
space retreats ever so quick
all stars on the move

in Europan slush
hot perfect radiation
starts sex in motion

☼

the constellations
like cave paintings in the sky
God's humble first steps

inside the capsule
they burn, so oxygen rich
dying before space

☼

stint wide the wormhole
fold flat the vast distances
sail the frozen light

melt bold Venera
seashell riding wax figure
acid waves of sky

☼

hiss of oxygen
the last sound that I will hear
as the tank ruptures

beautiful sunsets
in tertiary systems
three for every night

☼

burnup reentry
yellow streak across the sky
mankind's falling star

nova, nova, bang
a star death spectacular
blossoms elements

☼

all the humans wait
Laika looks down from above
chimpanzee suits up

Mars is calling us
inhospitable and cold
unfriendly siren

☼

asteroid coming
missiles finally let loose
man's final hour

settling dust falls
spacecraft disturbs ancient land
just to plant a flag

☼

oxygen burns bright
never to leave the capsule
dying before space

join the sixty mile-
high club, zero G sexy
mucking air filters

☼

jaunting to other planets
unprepared for the weather
no lukewarm porridge

ignition failure
aborting at the third stage
on the cusp of space

☼

exotic planets
stripping off their atmospheres
pole dancing axes

meteoric rise
as all the stars fall upward
back to outer space

☼

entering black hole
spaghettification, but
some sauce would be nice

atmospheric fire
the entire sky ignites
help…stromatolites

☼

a solitary
broadcast joins multitude
crying in the rain

ALIENS AND ROBOTS

robot overlords
the evolutionary
natural next step

<Θ>

anthropologist
robot digging up robots
searching for the past

virus colonize
killing the host in success
much like humankind

<Θ>

now galactic war
by the time we arrive
reasons forgotten

Venusian cloud
cities drift through atmosphere
on a balmy night

<Θ>

the sentient plants
are most furious about
vegetarians

laser gun misfire
hand melted around handle
they overtake us

<Θ>

a giant eyeball
looks at us through the glass cage
telepathic scream

a three fingered hand
different evolution
not human at all

<Θ>

take your breathing pills
my sky is foreign gasses
you'll drown in the air

radio signals
reaching through space to the Earth
xeno top-forty

<ϴ>

tendril reaches out
are we supposed to shake "hands?"
xenophobe faux pas

a great invasion
humanity's darkest hour
fallen to our knees

<Θ>

music for the eyes
a foreign race with no ears
hears architecture

alien takeover
new political structure
and strange new cuisine

<Θ>

I was abducted
by a need for attention
alienation

got the first contact
blues, didn't know what to say
or how to say it

<Θ>

menial labor
the robot supervisors
managing humans

milky white teardrops
fall from the android's face
it becomes human

<Ө>

little aliens
have taken over my brain
I'll do as they say

here come the robots
ruin humanities with
regurgitation

<Θ>

reruns across space
a repeatable pattern
intelligent life?

sentient plant life
light-eaters turning sugar
into alcohol

<Θ>

sentient machines
bitter about their makers
a need for power

my vision double
cannot tell the clones apart
or am I just drunk?

<\>

now the clone warfare
rises against itself
both sides are to lose

rogue planet
perpetual darkness
cold saucer-sized eyes

<Θ>

mini-black hole
harvester ants
outweigh dark matter

brain spores
lull me toward
fertile breeding grounds

<Θ>

robot servant strike
solar flare scabs
internet union network

SCIENCE

cosmic roll of dice
entropy still wins the game
all chance will wind down

❀

fighting entropy
always a losing battle
without a winner

growing, always more
parallel universes
still infinity

❁

warp drive folds spacetime
origami universe
unseen from outside

asymmetrical
a non-reversible flow
thermodynamic

❀

stuttering photons
spread across vast distances
at the end of time

chatGPT goes
the way of Dolly the sheep
forgotten folly

❁

the massless quanta
bends to the gravity well
lensing perfection

the earth's spin slowing
many gravity assists
not assistance now

❁

the ether not real
phlogiston not real either
ideas of the past

lasers in a sphere
eternal bounce in mirror
all waves collapse

❀

spheres of fire
in multitude they emit
radiant decay

grow and slow ether
equal and opposing force
cancels brilliantly

❁

forever the sun
falling inward and outward
thermonuclear

wave function collapse
observer interference
to uncertainty

❁

mirror universe
lean left amino acids
a different taste

the cosmic background
radiation, static thick
ubiquitous thoughts

<u>**Acknowledgements**</u>
Many of these poems first appeared in:
Accretion
Altered Realities
Dreams & Nightmares
Eccentric Orbits
Eldritch Science
Five Fleas
Pablo Lennis
Radon Journal
Scifaikuest
The Starlight SciFaiku Review

<u>**Other Books by Jean-Paul L. Garnier**</u>
Cardboard Spaceship
Black Line Trail
In Each Other's Arms
Proving Grounds
Garbage In, Gospel Out
Betelgeuse Dimming
Future Anthropology
Echo of Creation

About the Author

Jean-Paul L. Garnier is the owner of Space Cowboy Books bookstore and publishing house, producer of *Simultaneous Times Podcast* (2023 Laureate Award Winner, 2024 BSFA, Ignyte, and British Fantasy Award Finalist), and editor of the SFPA's *Star*Line* magazine. He is also the deputy editor-in-chief of *Worlds of IF & Galaxy* magazines. In 2024 he won the Laureate Award for Best Editor. He has written many books of poetry and science fiction.

https://spacecowboybooks.com/

9 798989 630844